That

Government

Smell

That Government Smell

A Romp Through the Swamp

By Raheem Cash

First Friday

The Blue Line slides smoothly into Farragut West station, then, as usual, it comes to a harsh stop, throwing passengers off balance.

R. regains his footing and exits the subway car shoulder to shoulder with the relieved rush hour crowd, all thankful for a rare delay-free morning.

It's Friday and R.'s first week at the Agency has gone well. Now, thanks to the small Metro miracle he has time to grab a baguette from his favorite bakery, Breadline, on Pennsylvania Avenue.

After tucking the baguette into his briefcase, R. heads to 18th Street and continues his stroll south towards the Agency's giant limestone building on F Street.

His positive energy lifts him up the low-sloping steps and through the main entrance where he encounters a second miracle. The security line is short. Actually, there is no line at all. *Strange*, he thinks.

R. pulls his ID out of his suit jacket pocket and shows it to the guard.

"Sorry, sir, you'll have to get a new ID," the young guard says.

"Jesus, Trevor, I've only been here a week! How can I possibly need a new ID already?"

"Sorry, sir, I really don't know."

Despite the outburst, R. likes Trevor. Unlike the other guards Trevor doesn't pretend that you are a stranger every morning.

Another guard, more experienced than Trevor, and therefore more ridiculous, rushes over to the scene as if he spotted a terrorist.

"Problem over here?"

"Nah, he's cool," Trevor says.

"Look, where do I get a new ID?"

"The Badge Office in the basement."

"Okay, can you let me through so I can go there?"

"No, someone has to escort you," the second guard barks.

"Someone? Who? Can you?"

"No, sir. Somebody has to come down and get you. The desk guard can call anybody you want."

2

R. takes a deep breath and slowly walks towards the desk guard. It dawns on him that no one else has entered the building during this fiasco. The marble-tiled lobby is eerily quiet. Today there are no clicking heels, no voices echoing.

The desk guard looks warily at him as he approaches. R. gives her the names of several people in his department. She makes the calls but no one answers.

"Where the hell is everybody?" R. asks.

"It's Friday," the guard says.

"So...," R. begins.

"So, why are you here trying to get in?"

"'Trying to get in'? I'm *here* trying to get to work and do my job."

"Oh," the guard says, rolling her eyes.

"Please I just need to get to the Badge Office."

"They're closed."

R. points to Trevor. "He didn't tell me that."

"He's kinda new."

"Okay, so the Badge Office is closed..."

"Yeah, it's Friday."

"So even if there were someone here to escort me, there'd be no place to go?" R. says.

"Hmm, no. I guess not."

"So what do I do? I can't get in."

"You can go home."

"Just go home?"

"Yeah. It's Friday."

R. of course does not 'just go home'. He's a thirty-four year-old former management consultant who has spent the last ten years solving problems for big corporations. He accepted this gig at the Agency because he believes more people like him should work for the government and make it better.

So R. is going to work, but apparently his government office is not the place to do it, at least not on Friday, the Federal Sabbath.

Everydays

Many weeks and IDs later R. walks up a flight of marble stairs from the Agency's lobby and enters a corridor marked *Office of Operational Program Services*. The sound of his footsteps echo off the arched ceilings as he walks past rows of tall solid wood doors.

The bright hall is a full city block long connecting the F Street and E Street sides of the building. R.'s office is towards the E Street end, aka the "back" of the building.

His walk takes him past the break room where he sees Aaron and Dave chatting.

Aaron is in his late forties and is an exceptional manager on R.'s staff who doesn't believe he receives enough exceptional treatment. Dave is also middle-aged. He's government lifer who is expert in seemingly everything except social skills.

R. checks his watch and notices that there's time for coffee before the weekly Director's meeting. But there's definitely no time for Dave

5

and Aaron's disgruntled federal employee routine.

R. continues to his office which is the last door on the left. Sunlight fills the room, nearly blinding him as he places his briefcase on the floor next to his bed-size desk.

He jogs to the break room hoping in vain that Dave and Aaron have gone. He'd love to ignore them but he is their new boss so the situation demands courtesy.

"Good morning, gentlemen," R. says as he grabs a Keurig pod and starts the machine.

Aaron, sensing an opportunity to bitch and moan says, "Hey, I bet you've been wondering why we always drink our coffee here and never at our desks."

R. couldn't imagine anything he'd care less about. "Uh, no, Aaron, I haven't actually, and I have to get to—"

"Well we just don't want to risk doing any work while drinking," Dave says.

"Ah, I see, you don't want to spill anything on your keyboard," R. says.

"No, nothing like that," Aaron

says. "We all pay for this coffee out of our own pockets. Anyplace else—like the firm you came from, for instance—the coffee would be free. But, oh no, not in the government. The taxpayer can't be asked to fund federal coffee. So I say, fine, I won't work for the taxpayer when I'm having my coffee."

****

R. escapes the Dave and Aaron show and arrives at the conference room where the other Directors are already gathered around a large oval table waiting for Kenny, the Executive Commissioner. R. sits in one of the $700 Herman Miller chairs next to Glen.

Glen is in his early sixties and was recruited from the private sector during a brief wave of so-called progressive government. Unfortunately it didn't take long for that wave to crash. Commissioner Franco demoted him and now he just clowns around in the bureaucratic circus he's dying to escape. Strategic doses of whiskey, a healthy paycheck, and constant thoughts of pending retirement keep Glen's spirits high.

"So you survived your first few months. I hope you're not too settled

in. We're moving offices next month,"
Glen says.

"Again?" The other Directors
groan.

"Where'd you hear that?" R.
asks.

Glen begins to answer but is
interrupted when Kenny and his
sycophant deputy Mike walk in.

Kenny is a dumb but lucky frat-
boy type. Like all of the highest-
ranking people at the Agency, Kenny is
a man of below-average height and
intelligence. Mike, like all of the
Deputies, is a slightly taller, more
seasoned man who sacrificed his
dignity on the altar of advancement
ages ago.

Kenny jumps into his chair and
swivels like a three year old. "Hey,
hey, everybody, good morning! How's it
going? Everybody good? Good weekend?
Good, good!"

Kenny, adding a finger drum roll
to his swing finally starts the
meeting. "Okay, okay. So, it's the
staff meeting. That time again. Great
to hear you all had a good weekend.
Yep. Yep. Good. Good."

Kenny, not missing a beat or
swivel, turns to R.

8

"Speaking of staff meetings, Mike tells me you haven't had enough staff meetings."

Kenny swivels to Mike, who is stroking his salt and pepper goatee and peering through small, round spectacles.

"Mike, that's what you said this morning right? When I texted you at three a.m.? Or was it my 5 a.m. text? Oh wait, no it was during breakfast a half hour ago. Man I haven't had enough coffee."

Kenny stops swiveling and continues to school R. "Staff meetings are essential dude, just like this one. So you gotta make them happen man. Okay? Good. Next item. Budget cuts."

Everyone groans, except R. He's already seen plenty of opportunities to save money at the Agency. Budget cuts are definitely justified.

Kenny continues, "Yep, we knew these cuts were coming and they will be worse than last year. So we must talk about each of your programs. There will be big cuts. Cuts in programs, cuts in travel, conference cancellations. No one program is more critical than any other; everything is

9

on the chopping block."

Mike leans over and whispers in Kenny's ear. Kenny smiles and whispers, "No, not *your* programs, dude. Don't worry, I got your back."

Kenny continues. "The Commissioner expects us all to do our part. The good news is that Jeb Stanly the Regional Commissioner of the West has some ideas on how we can cope with the cuts. We'll be reviewing his plans when we head out to Vegas for the Big Agency Conference."

"The Vegas Conference isn't on the chopping block?" R. asks.

R. is sure someone has slipped a noise-canceling headset over his ears. Dead silence surrounds him and he foolishly fills the vacuum.

"I mean, given the serious budget cuts you were just talking about, it would seem that such a huge conference…," R. continues.

Now I must be underwater, R. thinks. He hears nothing but can see the other Directors' heads shaking, pitying the drowning man. R. is not sure how long he was under but eventually his ears pop and he hears Kenny's voice.

"Well, hey, thanks, everyone.

That's all for today. Oh, and next time we'll talk about the Move."

Everyone stands and gathers their mugs and government-issued iPhones. R. takes a final sip of coffee from his mug and follows everyone out of the conference room, avoiding eye contact, which isn't difficult given that no one dares to look at him, he who dared to suggest sacrificing the Conference Cow.

* * * *

R. stands at the first of seven urinals in a large restroom bathed in sunlight shining in from enormous windows. The urinals are the old-fashioned kind that go all the way down to the floor and have no partitions.

R. uses this moment to clear his mind as well as his bladder. He looks up, eyes closed, and breathes gently, relishing his only sanctuary at the Agency. The bathroom is empty and quiet, just what he needs.

"Hey! Hey!"

Brett, a fellow Director, announces his arrival and, social butterfly that he is, flutters over to the urinal right next to R. who flinching from the bug.

"Ready to fight for your box?" Brett says.

R., still hopeful that peace might break out again, mutters, "My box? Yeah, yeah. Sure."

"You don't know what I'm talking about do you? You heard about the Move, right?"

"Yeah, I've heard about the Move, but I have to finish my Strategic Plan for the Commissioner. That's the only thing on my mind. We're moving. So what?"

R. flushes, zips up, and walks to the row of sinks, leaving Brett at the urinal.

Brett, flabbergasted and not quite done peeing, drips and zips hurriedly and flushes hard. He dashes to the sink next to R.

"'So what?' I'll tell you so what. When there's a move lots of boxes are shuffled around, and sometimes a few get lost, or stolen."

"Brett, nobody wants my stuff. I haven't been here long enough to really have anything to take."

Brett, becoming apocalyptic, reaches into his pocket, yanks out a piece of paper and fervently unfolds

12

it in R.'s face.

"I'm talking about your *box*! On the *org chart*!" Brett says while stabbing the paper with his fingers. R. merely glances at the sheet which shows the Agency's convoluted structure.

Brett shoves the paper back into his pocket. "That box is your piece of the Agency pie! And every move is a chance for someone to steal a slice."

As Brett implodes, R. looks in the mirror to adjust his tie and sees Uncle Sam walk in and go to a urinal. It's *the* Uncle Sam, tall, long white hair, wearing red and white striped pants and a top hat. Uncle Sam lets loose a loud, Niagara-worthy stream of pee. R. turns around quickly but sees nothing.

Brett notices R.'s movement but does not see Uncle Sam. "Yep, you'd better get used to looking over your shoulder. The Move is really about who gets shitty space, who loses staff, and who loses their box," Brett says.

R., still shaken by the Uncle Sam appearance, gives a wary look to the urinals as he dries his hands and tries to reorient himself.

R. follows Brett out of the

restroom and they head in opposite directions. After turning a corner on the 19th Street side of the building R. trips over something and nearly falls. He looks back and sees Uncle Sam leaning against the wall smoking marijuana like a high school punk. He blows smoke in the air and turns towards R.

"Oops. Sorry about that. You should watch your step," Uncle Sam says as he turns and slowly walks away, fading with every step until he completely disappears.

* * * *

R. attempts redemption by fulfilling Kenny's mandate to have more staff meetings.

He walks across the hall to a door directly opposite his office. Behind this door is a warren of grayish-blue walled cubicles where his staff toils in perpetual cloudy day gloom thanks to the tall gray file cabinets blocking ornate windows.

R. has to stretch his neck a bit to confirm that all of the heads are in place.

"Good morning everyone. Glad you're all here," R. says to the heads

14

which have now tilted upwards.

R. continues, now speaking to eyes and chins, "Apparently I've been neglecting an important ritual, staff meetings. I don't want to go overboard so for now we'll start with monthly meetings."

The eyes shine brightly and the chins nod approvingly.

"To be efficient I want to make them lunch meetings. I'll send out an email with the schedule."

At this R. sees eyebrows furrow, some eyes turn fierce, others flash with utter confusion.

"You want us to...*work* during lunch?" asks Aaron.

R. expects nothing less from Aaron.

"Well, it's work but it's also a good way to get the team together informally."

Dave chimes in, "I'm having a hard time with this possible mixing of personal and work-related conversation. Are you proposing lunch or a work meeting? This is very complicated."

Aaron adds "Yeah, it is. I'm not sure it's legal, and even if it is, we still have lunch rights that must be

15

respected."

R. finds himself appreciating Aaron's talent for pointing out the bureaucratic disease that infects every attempt at efficiency. *The problem is people like Aaron and Dave don't want to be cured*, R. thinks.

"Okay," R. relents, "I will schedule a meeting later so we can figure out a meeting schedule."

"You can't believe you just spoke that sentence, can you?" Darcy says to R. as she laughs.

Darcy is in her late twenties, R.'s youngest staff member. She's a smart, spunky, petite woman with deep Chicago-Greek roots. Unlike R. Darcy did not enter government to fix it, she thought it was already set up for someone like her to come in and do good things. Instead after only one year on the job she finds herself surrounded by what she calls the Walking Fed, co-workers who have been at the Agency so long their souls are dead. They are either unable to see what's wrong or they are infected with apathy.

After laughing a bit more she says to R., "You thought this would be easy, right?"

* * * *

Kenny paces excitedly behind his large desk. The office is filled with flags, mugs, and other items bearing the letters for Delta Upsilon Mu, his college fraternity.

Mike sits on a sofa stroking his goatee. His eyes follow Kenny as one would a tennis ball.

"I can't believe it! This is sweet!" Kenny exclaims.

"It's a lot of power and a big—" Mike begins.

"Yeah! The power. For the first time I get to decide the fate of so many," Kenny says.

"Responsibility," Mike continues.

"Responsibility?! Come on, don't be such a downer. This is fun! Moving people around and shit. It's like being God. I get to giveth and taketh!" Kenny shouts.

Kenny's mood suddenly darkens, he plops down in his leather chair with a look of dread.

"But I have to get this right. I've got to show the Commissioner that he made the best choice putting me in this position," Kenny says.

17

"You're the best," Mike reassures him.

"I gotta show that I can make the big decisions, handle the tough calls."

"You're the toughest."

"The Commissioner has to know that I belong behind this big desk."

"You're the biggest behind."

"What do I do Mike!"

* * * *

R. leaves his office and walks down the hallway and turns left to proceed down yet another block-long corridor lined with doors on either side. Eventually he reaches the door he seeks and enters an open area of low-partitioned cubicles with private offices on the sides. Unlike his staff, this group works in eternal daylight, yet he's never noticed any difference in productivity, effectiveness, or happiness that light is supposed to bring.

He approaches a large desk in the middle where Diana, the admin assistant, sits among photos of her chubby grandchildren and a safari of tiny stuffed animals.

"Good morning, Diana. How are

you?"

Diana, not looking up, says, "I'm fine, sir. What can I do for you?"

"I still need to order some office supplies. How do I—"

Diana, who is no more than 5'3", suddenly lifts up a huge, phonebook-sized catalog and drops it down with a loud thud. Papers fly off her desk.

"Here ya go. Just pick what you want and I'll place the order."

R. flips through the book with a slight frown.

"Diana, none of this stuff is green."

"Sure it is. You can get almost any color."

"No, I mean *green* like recyclable, non-toxic, good for the environment."

Diana slowly turns her head toward R., annoyed as hell.

"Well, I don't know if we can get any of that stuff. This ain't Whole Foods."

"Okay, well, I'll just order online," R. says as he carefully backs away.

"Now hold on! You can't just order government supplies from

anywhere. They've got to come from an approved source."

"I'm not ordering an F-16!"

"Look! You are violating the regulations. Now if you want to get yourself some contraband, you go right ahead, but don't expect me to place the order. I'm not going to jail because of you."

Diana turns back to her monitor while R. walks away bewildered, again. He escapes through one of the doors back into the main corridor.

His relief is short-lived. As he walks he notices Glen beckoning him in the distance.

As R. approaches, Glen cheerfully puts an arm around his shoulders like a car salesman.

"How would you like to have a personal secretary instead of dealing with Diana?"

"Diana's okay, she's just a product of the system, that's all. I'll fix that."

They enter Glen's office. It is larger than R.'s but lacks a window. R. sits on a plush leather sofa while Glen settles into a high-backed chair behind the desk.

"Your consultant voodoo can't

fix Diana. Anyway I used to have a personal secretary before I got screwed during the last Move."

"How? I mean, what did the Move have to do with it?" R. says.

"Everything of course! Anyway, her name's Maureen. Since I lost her three years ago we haven't found anything for her to do."

"Three years—," R. says.

"Do you want her? If nobody takes her this time I don't think she'll survive The Move," Glen says.

"What do you mean 'survive The Move'? What's with everybody around here? You'd think changing offices was a life or death—"

"It is! Commissioner Franco uses these moves to reward and punish. Your little boss Kenny is a newly anointed ass-kisser who is definitely going to do his best to please Franco, and that means you're in for a nasty Move. You'd better prepare yourself."

R. rolls his eyes. "Whatever. Look, what can this Maureen do? Is she good with PowerPoint, Excel? Maybe she could help me with my Strategic Plan."

"She's a typist."

"A typist?"

"A typist."

21

"A typist?"

"Yep."

"Jesus, Glen, it's the twenty-first century. Is that all she can do?"

"Now wait a minute. I didn't say she could type."

"Oh no. You're kidding."

"Oh no, I'm not."

"How can that be..."

"Is it that shocking?"

"Depends on what planet you're on, Glen. In some places painters paint, actors act, judges judge. But apparently here on Planet Government—"

"Okay, okay. Guess I'd better not tell you that she makes seventy-five grand a year."

Glen cracks up and Uncle Sam, visible only to R., jumps up from the sofa, dances, and cheers, "Woohoo!"

* * * *

R. and his staff step off an elevator and find themselves in an open, bright white corridor. White leather lounge chairs dot the path. There are cubicles with low white partitions allowing everyone to see and breathe. Daylight illuminates the entire space and not a sound can be heard.

"It's like they invented white noise here." Monique says.

Monique just turned fifty but looks thirty. She's a former gymnast who has maintained her shape. She has been in the government since her twenties and has established herself as a force to be reckoned with.

"I've never been on this floor before. Where the hell are we?" says Dave.

"This floor had the only available conference room. I think all of the architects are on this floor." Darcy says.

"Oh, that's right," Monique says. "The Chief Architect was allowed to design his own wing. And this is what he does. Feels like a psychiatric ward."

Eventually they reach the conference room. It is filled with state-of-the-art IT and A/V equipment.

"The best taxpayer money can buy," Monique says.

They slide into plush white chairs around the oblong white table. Leafy green plants rest in the corners of the room.

R. says, "Okay, everyone, as I

23

said earlier, we need to set up a day and time for our monthly staff meetings. I've suggested that we hold them during lunch but apparently there are some complications that I did not foresee. So we're here to work this out, quickly I hope."

"Good luck," Darcy mouths silently to R.

Aaron raises his hand. "Actually I'll have to check with the union on the monthly thing."

"You do that, Aaron. Now, I am thinking that Thursdays would be a perfect day and if lunch is impossible then we can do 10:30."

"I get every other Thursday off. So if a meeting falls on one of my off Thursdays, I won't be there," Dave says.

"Thanksgiving is always on a Thursday, you know," says Monique.

"Well, we can schedule it early in each month, so that would automatically avoid Thanksgiving."

"The first two weeks of every month I'm entitled to work from home. This meeting upsets that schedule," Aaron says.

"Oh, but you can get comp time for the meeting," Dave added.

"But you're *working* at home, right? The meeting is part of work. You can dial in," R. says.

Darcy jumps in. "Actually, Aaron, you're eligible for reimbursement for the phone call…"

R. shoots Darcy an incredulous "Et tu Brute?" look.

"I'm just pointing out the rule. Mere technicality," she says, smiling.

"Perhaps you should consider working in the office on the one Thursday we have a meeting," R. suggests.

"Coming in on those Thursdays would require a Change of Work Schedule Form and you'd have to reimburse me for travel costs," Aaron says.

"Travel! To where?"

"Well, he has to get to the office that day," Dave says.

"It's his commute to work!"

"Well, not during those two weeks it's not. Since he would normally be working from home that day, 'work' is at home and the office is away from 'work'," Dave explains.

"But—" R. starts, but Monique cuts in.

"Actually I just remembered that

on the Thursdays that I work, I only work two hours so I won't even be here after 10:00."

For once it's R.'s turn to fall silent as the cacophony of excuses swirls around him. He eventually summons the will to speak once more.

"Okay, okay. I get it. We've taken nearly an hour so far. I'll figure something out and email a list of options and we'll see which one gets the most votes."

This appeared to satisfy everyone especially since it was nearly lunchtime. The staff filed out of the room with a sense of accomplishment leaving an exhausted R. behind as he lay his bald brown head on the smooth, cool white table.

★ ★ ★ ★

The Blue Line slowly takes a curve as it leaves the National Airport station. R. sits with his head leaning against the window looking out at the airplanes on the runway. Calvin is seated next to him reading the *New York Times* on his iPhone.

Calvin is a tall white-haired gentleman who has been with the Agency for thirty years. He has a distinguished and slightly weathered look and could easily be a 19th century Supreme Court justice. He dispenses wisdom in the manner of an aged Al Pacino.

R. turns to Calvin. "How do you do it?"

"It, what?" Calvin says.

"Thirty years. Thirty years with the Agency?"

"Oh that. Sure you don't mean 'why'?" Calvin says.

"'Why' would be good to know but the question I've been asking myself lately is 'how', and I've only been here a few months. I mean, you're not one of the 'Get In Stay In' idiots."

"Get in, stay in?" Calvin says.

"Yeah. Dave and Aaron shared more of their wisdom with me. They explained how people get in to government and just coast along doing nothing and get paid more and more."

"Oh, so, they described themselves."

"Basically, yeah," R. replies laughing. "But seriously, they said people will put up with all kinds of bullshit but they 'Stay-In' no matter what."

"That happens," Calvin says.

"Yes but we've got brilliant people like you and complete imbeciles like Kenny. I sit in meetings with people supposedly in charge of things and they are like zombies. Zombies shitting their pants, scared to make decisions because they're afraid of being fired. Fired from a job they can't be fired from! They just sit there and rot, doing nothing. Changing nothing. Not even trying. You survived this for thirty years!"

Calvin gives R. a solemn look. "It's not for everyone."

* * * *

Kenny is curled up on his office sofa reading a book. Mike enters carrying three management books, *Being a New Leader*, *Making Smart Decisions*, and *Managerial Judgment 101*.

"Hey I've found these for you. They might help with The Move decisions."

Mike puts the books down on Kenny's desk while Kenny continues to read. "Man this is awesome!" Kenny says.

"What is that?" Mike asks.

Kenny shuts the book and straightens up triumphantly on the

sofa.

"It's the solution Mike! No need for those books of yours. My brothers from Delta Upsilon Mu gave me this!"

Kenny holds up the book for Mike to see... *Amazing Hazing: Tips for Deciding Who Belongs*.

★ ★ ★ ★

R. works intently at his computer. One screen is covered with an Excel spreadsheet; the other displays a PowerPoint Presentation. His desk lamp is on now due to the storm darkened afternoon sky. Rumbles of thunder can be heard in the distance but below that sound he hears soft sighs coming from the hall.

R. often leaves his door open. It's a good management practice, most of the time. After a while the sighs become grunts and R. turns to see Dave hovering at the door's threshold.

"You got a minute, boss?" Dave says.

Dave is annoying, there I've said it, R. says to himself.

"Yeah Dave, sure, come in. I've made some headway with my Strategic Plan."

Dave plops heavily into a chair and sighs. "Hopefully I'm not speaking out of turn. People have been talking about a Move. I don't know who started the rumor…"

"It's no secret, Dave. Yes, there is a Move. What about it?"

"Well I just want you to know that I don't really have a preference for anything. I'm not like these other people who want big offices. That stuff doesn't matter to me."

"That's a good attitude."

"You're not going to give me a smaller office anyway, right? Not that it matters to me of course. I can work from anywhere. That's why I don't need a window office."

"Really."

"There are only what, six window offices?"

"No, I think five," R. says. He knows there are six but the passive aggression is killing him; toying with Dave is merely self-defense.

"Oh, no, you're forgetting the one over by—"

"So you've seen the floor plans?"

"No. No, no. I didn't see them, really. I mean, some papers were on

Kenny's secretary's desk—"

At this moment Darcy walks into the office and hands Dave sheets of paper that are obviously copies of floor plans.

"Here. You left these at the printer."

Dave recoils as if she were handing him a snake. "Those are not mine!"

"The bottom of each sheet says 'Dave'—"

"Oh, oh, yeah that's right. Kenny's secretary was having trouble with her printer, so I—"

"Yeah, whatever," Darcy cuts in. "Next time save some trees and steal copies from the conference room like everyone else did." She points at R. "Our dear leader is an environmentalist, you know."

Darcy smiles at R. as she carefully steps over Dave's legs and sits on a side sofa. She crosses her legs and leans back as if she were lounging at an old friend's house. R. smiles back shaking his head in mock annoyance.

"Look guys I have to finish up this Strategic Plan."

"You know you're the only

Director bothering with that," Darcy says.

"Perhaps. But that's why I'm here, to demonstrate how things ought to be done. 'Be the change you want to see in the world', that's the motto I'm following."

Darcy laughs. "I'm sorry. It's always funny when you talk like that. Sweet actually."

"Thanks. I think. But seriously I've got to…"

"I just came by to give you this book." Darcy hands R. Sun Tzu's *The Art of War*. "Brett said it would help you with The Move."

"Jesus!" R. exclaims. "Doesn't anyone have real work to do? This Move crap is ridiculous."

Darcy says, "Well I wasn't here for the last Move but it sounds scary. I'm not sure what will happen to me if you lose the battle."

"Battle? Happen to you? What…"

"Yeah. There's some kind of contest thing Kenny is cooking up for new Directors. That's what I heard anyway. Sounds like it's a big deal."

R. takes a deep breath and slowly blows out as he leans back in his chair. He looks at the book

solemnly, nods and says, "Yes. I see
now."

Moving Days

Brett and R. enter a conference room and find Glen standing around a large table with the other Directors. A war room has been created. The table is covered with the building's floor plans and figurines are set in battle positions. On one wall is a huge sheet of paper showing a blow-up of the Agency's org chart.

R. looks around the room with a confused expression. "Are we invading Canada?"

"No, this is a real fight," Brett replies.

Next Kenny and Mike arrive carrying casino dice sticks. Kenny loudly clasps his hands together and rubs them excitedly. "Okay! Everyone here?"

Kenny bounces excitedly on his toes and continues to rub his hands. "This is gonna be fun! My first Reorganization as an Executive Commissioner. This is what it's all about!"

"Reorganization? I thought we

were preparing to move," R. says.

R. is hit with that underwater deafness again.

Mike finally says, "It's really simple. The only way to get funding approved for moves to new office space and get new furniture is to plan a Reorg. And we can't get approval to do a Reorg unless we submit plans to move, even if we don't plan to move. That's just the process."

"Got it?" Kenny asks, miffed at the lost momentum.

R., like a drowning man looking up from the abyss at a panicked crowd, can see everyone silently screaming at him, "Say 'yes'! Please say 'yes'!". This time he wants to be rescued so he merely nods his head 'yes' so they can move on.

Kenny exclaims, "Okay! Let's do it." He walks over to Deena, a sad, kind, frumpy, overweight woman.

"Deena! Let's see, you have a corner office on the fourth floor now. You know, I think you can handle an inside office on the seventh floor. Don't worry; we're getting good space up there. You'll like it."

"But I won't have a window," Deena mutters.

"No but you'll be near the vending machines. No views but lots to chew. Ha! That was funny! Gotta love that, right! See, Uncle Kenny's got your back dude!"

Mike goes to the table, picks up a figurine and places it on the 7th floor's plan. Kenny paces a bit then stops in front of Kirkland, another Director whose natural appearance serves as a 'Kick Me' sign for people like Kenny.

"You know, Kirkland, I think we'll finally get you out of a cube and into an office."

Kenny goes to the table and picks up a casino dice stick so he can push some figurines. "So we'll just move you and your staff to the sixth…"

As Kenny begins to push the group of figurines across the floor plan, Mike whispers in his ear. Kenny perks up.

"Oh crap! That's right. Yo, Kirkland. You haven't come to any of my voluntary breakfast meetings, bro. So you won't be joining your staff on the sixth floor."

Kenny picks up one figurine from the group he previously pushed and places it back in its original spot, which is now an empty space.

Kirkland protests. "I'm a vegan and you only have eggs, bacon..."

"Hey, c'mon, dude, don't play the race card. That ain't cool."

Kirkland, confused, looks at his white hand. "What? But..."

Kenny turns to Mike. "Mike, who's been coming to my breakfasts?"

"Bev is always there."

"Oh! Bev, the intern on your team. Yeah, she's hot—I mean cool. Very cool. Let's put her up on six. Kirkland, your team likes Bev, right?"

"Yes, but if you just served some tofu eggs or—"

"Hey, no problem, dude. You and your kind are always welcome at breakfast. Come when you can, okay? Cool. This is good. A good leadership opportunity for Bev."

"Leadership? But she's an intern," R. mistakenly says out loud.

"What is your point exactly?" Kenny says with annoyance. "Kirkland's former staff are moving to the sixth floor. Kirkland is going down to the basement. You think it makes sense to leave the people on the sixth floor without a leader? Is that the way you guys did things in the private sector?

37

Jeez!"

Kirkland shudders and begins to blubber. "Blueberry bars, quinoa porridge—"

"Dude, now you're speaking in tongues. Calm down."

Kirkland runs out of the room as Mike goes to the org chart on the wall and writes a large red 'X' over Kirkland's name and pencils in 'Bev'.

Kenny rubs his hands together excitedly and bounces on his toes.

"All righty it's time for the main event. Man I've always wanted to do this. Where are the new guys?"

R. and Mark, who is on the opposite side of the table, raise their hands.

"Okay newbies. We've got some primo space upstairs for your departments, and it could be yours."

Kenny pauses to laugh then continues. "Well it can only be one of yours. I thought long and hard about how to make this decision and figured you guys should earn your spot."

R. and Mark exchange mutual 'WTF!' glances.

Kenny continues. "Consider it a rite of passage gentleman."

Kenny walks over to the table

and picks up another dice stick. He uses the sticks to gather the figurines and position two groups opposite each other.

"Okay, the goal is to get your team over here to the best spot," Kenny says as he points to an area marked "PRIMO" on the floor plan.

"So guys, how are you gonna make that happen? What's the game plan?"

R. and Mark exchange glances again.

"Oh wait, I forgot to give you these," Kenny says as he hands R. and Mark one dice stick each.

"Now, if you want your team to have that awesome space upstairs you'll have to earn it. Now's the time. Earn it!"

Mark and R. each hold their dice sticks and look around the room. Then they look at each other. They have no idea what they're supposed to do. R. looks down at the table. Kenny is bouncing on his toes manically.

"Come on guys! Let's go! Whose gonna get that primo space? Earn it! Earn it!"

Mark takes his dice stick and starts to gently push his team's figurines towards "PRIMO".

39

R., with a swift, ninja-like move, whacks Mark's arm with his dice stick and then quickly pushes his team into the "PRIMO" space.

"Ow! Fuck!" Mark screams, holding his arm.

The other Directors gasp. Kenny explodes. "Whoo! Man that was awesome! Damn!"

★ ★ ★ ★

A few days later Aaron peeks into R.'s office. "Boss, you got a minute? I heard about the Move, or Reorg, or whatever they're calling it this time."

"Nothing is final yet. Jesus!"

Aaron, who is wearing sneakers with his suit, jumps excitedly into R.'s sofa.

"Good. That means there's still time to sort things out."

"Oh I think he's already done that." Darcy says as she happens to pass by.

"What? What are you…" R. starts.

"*You* know, you're the Whack a Mole expert, or should I say Whack a Mark?" Darcy says before she cracks up.

"How did you—" R. begins.

Aaron says, "Oh that's why Mark's arm is—"

"What about Mark's arm?" R. says.

"Way to go boss, we must really be getting some good space," Aaron says.

Darcy manages to stop laughing for a moment. "Nice to have a leader that really fights for you right."

"Look, enough. Aaron you wanted something?" R. says as Darcy continues on her way.

"Well, to start with, the name of my department. With all of these changes happening it's a good time to add the word 'experts' to the name."

"You want to be the Department of Technical Services *Experts*?"

"Right."

"Aaron, we've had this conversation. On my first day, in fact."

"Glad you remembered."

"I remember, but I have not changed my view on the matter. Aren't we all supposed to be experts at what we do? Why shouldn't every department add 'experts' to their name? And what would 'experts' imply about departments that do not use that word?

Are they presumed to be groups of idiots?"

"Well, you know, some of them are," Aaron says.

R., knowing all too well how true this is, can't believe he just torpedoed his own argument. But fortunately another visitor rescues him.

Monique pokes her head in to R.'s office. "You guys having a staff powwow without me?"

"Definitely nothing *wow* going on here. More like pow-pow," R. says as he points a finger gun at his head. "I'm almost dead. Want to take your shot?"

"No, I just wanted a quick word about the Move..."

"Pow!" R. shouts as he slumps in his chair.

* * * *

The staff cubicle pen has given way to chaos. Boxes and dumpsters bulge with bureaucratic artifacts. Employees are packing, sorting, and trashing papers, binders, and books.

The towers of file cabinets have been removed, so for the first time in decades natural light shines through.

Now it looks like a place they should be moving *in* to instead of out.

R.'s office in contrast is an oasis of calm yet covered in darkness. He sits at his computer working with boxes neatly stacked against the windows.

Darcy, wearing jeans and a blouse with sleeves rolled up, stops by.

"Very nice. Had your Oompa Loompas pack for you?"

"Just being efficient," R. says, smiling.

"That's easy when you haven't been here a million years. You know, somebody actually had a Sony Walkman in their drawer!"

"That's what happens when you can't fire anybody."

Darcy flashes him a harsh look.

"Just saying," R. responds

"You should come see how crazy it is out there amongst us common folk."

R. stands up and stretches. "You're right. A leader has to be seen amongst his people."

"Sure you have time? Finished that Strategic Plan of yours?"

It's R.'s turn to flash a harsh

43

look.

"Just saying," Darcy replies.

R. and Darcy go to the staff cubicle zone. They approach Monique's cube and find it blockaded by large dumpsters filled with thick binders and paper.

Monique is busily moving items around, it's hard to tell whether she's packing or unpacking.

"Oh hi boss. Thanks for getting us such a good spot upstairs. How'd you pull that off? I thought we were screwed with you being a new Director and all," Monique says.

"You don't know…," Darcy starts.

R., cuts in, "I did what I had to do for my staff. So, you're welcome. That's all."

Monique, oblivious to R.'s discomfort continues, "I heard the other new Director, what's his name, Mark something, took a beating…"

"Hey, you know sometimes things are exaggerated," R. says.

Mark, wearing one arm in a sling and holding a coffee mug in his other hand, happens to walk by at this moment. He sees R. and scurries away in panic.

R. calls after him, "Mark wait!

Look I'm sorry. I didn't mean to…I didn't have a choice…"

"Wow, that definitely looked exaggerated," Darcy says.

Monique looks at R. with wide eyes and a look of awe and admiration. "Oooh, no, did you…wow!"

R. replies, "Look I'm not proud of it you know."

"You really did fight for us!"

Darcy and Monique cheer together, "What a guy!"

R., desperate to change the subject says, "Monique, do you need help with anything?"

"If you want, you can start taking these binders to the large recycling bin."

"What are these, anyway?" R. asks as he picks up a binder and leans over to look at some of the others.

"Oh, those are just a bunch of Old Initiatives."

"Old Initiatives?"

"Yeah, look. See, this one is from the 2005 Customer Service Improvement Initiative. That was actually fun. We had four big training conferences. Miami, San Diego, Honolulu, and New Orleans. Every employee had to attend."

"So what happened?" R. asks

"To what? Oh, to the Customer Service Improvement Initiative?"

"Yeah. Any 'improvement' after all of that money spent?"

"Not really. Didn't matter anyway. A new Commissioner came in 2009 so that was that."

"What do you mean?"

Darcy suppresses laughter as she prepares for what she knows is about to hit R.

Monique replies, "In 2009 the new Commissioner launched a Client Service Improvement Initiative."

Monique hands R. a different binder.

R. reads the title and says, "Sounds like the same..."

"No, this was for 'Clients'. Not 'Customers'."

"And the difference is?"

"The new Commissioner preferred 'Clients,' that's the difference. I think we're back to saying 'Customers,' though."

"So this binder is all the stuff from the 2009 training on the 'new' initiative which was 'new' because it had a new title?"

"Yep," Monique continues. "But

the 2009 trainings were not as much fun for me. They were held in ski resorts, and I don't ski. But the chalets were nice."

Monique picks up another binder. "Oh, wow, I never thought I'd see this again. Hey, Dave, Aaron, come here."

Dave and Aaron hurry over, knocking a few items over as they come but no one seems to care.

"Look," Monique says excitedly, "I found the 2006 Agency Reinvention Convention binder."

They gather around and start going through pages of org charts while R. looks on.

Dave says, "It's the book that changed everything: new org structure, new departments, new offices. Lasted about two years."

Aaron chimes in. "After this Reorg—I mean Move, or, whatever—everything will be the same as it was then."

"Why did it change in the first place?" R. asks. "Hasn't the Agency been doing the same thing since 1949? How many reorgs have there been?"

"How many reorgs since 1949 or just in the last three years?"

R. looks at Darcy with a 'should

I go on?' look. Her eyes give a clear answer.

"Never mind," R. says.

* * * *

Monday arrives and the Move appears to have been a success. The new office area is bright and filled with sleek, modern furniture. The scene is like a Christmas morning with employees opening boxes excitedly, eager to retrieve their books and useless files.

Brett walks down a side aisle and stops by Dave's new office. Actually it is more of a nook than an office. There are no windows but on the wall hangs a large Microsoft "Windows + Office" poster.

Brett catches Dave's eye and gives him a thumbs up. "Nice digs! Way to go."

Dave gives Brett the finger.

Brett continues and slows as he passes Aaron's office. He notices a piece of tape next to his nameplate with the word "Expert" written in large red letters.

Brett proceeds to R.'s office. R. is already at work in his new space, everything has been unpacked

and put away neatly. He now has a
second door allowing him to enter the
staff area without stepping into the
main hallway. The boomerang-shaped
desk fits nicely in the corner, so he
can take advantage of both window
views and still have something between
him and any visitors.

His monitor proudly displays a
PowerPoint slide titled "Five-Year
Budget Plan" with some graphs.

"That was quick," Brett says.

"I came in over the weekend to
unpack. So today I think I'll get this
Strategic Plan done."

"Oh really? You're doing that?"
He then notices R.'s computer. "Hey,
how did you get your computer and
phone hooked up over the weekend?"

"What do you mean? I just hooked
them up, nothing to it."

Brett is suddenly nervous. He
starts to shake and sputters, "Well,
okay, uh, good luck with the, with
your uh, Strategic Plan. I gotta run.
You'll be at the gym later, right?"

"Sure, probably around.." R.
begins to reply but Brett has
disappeared.

Moments later a shabbily dressed
stout man walks by R.'s office slowly

49

and looks in with a serious face. Shortly after that another shabbily dressed man, this one bald, tall, and bouncer-like, walks by his second door very slowly.

After five minutes the two ogres appear again, this time both standing at the second door. As R. looks towards them a short, thin man stops at the entrance of R.'s main office door. He's wearing what appears to be an Armani suit and looks a bit like Silvio Berlusconi.

"Can I help you?" R. asks.

All of the men enter the office without a word. The ogres amble menacingly to R.'s bookshelves. The Armani man approaches the desk.

"Sir, sorry to bother you. We were just wondering if you needed any assistance."

"Assistance with…?"

"You know, moving your things, setting things up. It was a pretty big Move."

R. ponders his response as the goons begin to take things off the shelves, peer at them quizzically, then place them down roughly.

Armani man continues. "We just want you to know that we're here all week to help you, and your staff, in any way."

"I appreciate that. My staff might need some help out there but, as you can see, I'm all set here."

"No problems? Your computer and telephone working okay?"

The bouncer fiddling with one of R.'s favorite African statuettes, adds, "A lot of things can happen. Can go wrong I mean."

The stout ruffian, inspecting R.'s espresso machine says, "Things can happen to your stuff before and *after* a move like this. We don't want it to happen to you."

"Thanks. My computer is fine, the phone is good," R. says as he ponders the 'it' that could happen to him.

"Okay sir. You have a good day," Mr. Armani says.

★ ★ ★ ★

R. stands squished in a Metro Blue Line car headed for Alexandria. Next to him is Calvin.

"So, how are you surviving this mess I got you into? Any regrets?" Calvin asks.

"No, I'm not ready to run back

51

to consulting if that's what you mean." R. replies.

"Government is a challenge but I'm up to it. Hell I even got something done this week, I finished my Strategic Plan."

"Excellent. And your corpse is not floating in the Potomac River. That's even better"

"What?" R. says.

Calvin laughs. "It seems you've pissed off some powerful people."

"What? Who?"

"The union boys."

"The who? Oh, those goons who interrupted me today?"

"Yes," Calvin replies. "It's their job to hook up everyone's computer and telephones whenever there's a Move."

"Jesus! This is so insane."

Calvin cracks up. "And you did it over the weekend, you cost them overtime!"

R. shakes his head slowly, feeling bemused, confused, and yet somewhat amused.

"Ah screw it," Calvin continues. "There's not enough toilet paper in the world to deal with Uncle Sam's bullshit."

R. looks around the Metro car nervously half expecting to see Uncle Sam writing graffiti or something. But he only sees the grim faces of his fellow commuters silently praying for an uneventful journey home.

* * * *

Delays on the Blue Line have forced R. and Calvin onto the Yellow Line for the morning commute. R. likes this line because it provides a glimpse of the monuments as it crosses over the Potomac. A view of a beautiful Washington from the outside, such a relief from what he sees inside everyday.

The passengers are quiet and evenly split between those reading and those staring out the window.

"Choose your battles," Calvin suddenly says to R.

"Fine I can choose them but it would be nice to win some," R. says.

R. returns his gaze to the Jefferson Memorial then back to Calvin.

"Have you won any?"

"I like to think that I've helped move the Agency forward over the years," Calvin says.

"You mean with all of the projects and initiatives? Well last week I learned how that works. Nothing lasts more than three or four years. You win only to fight the same battle again. And again," R. says as he turns towards the window which now provides a black view of the tunnel. "That isn't winning in my book."

"You know the saying two steps forward one step back?" Calvin replies.

"Yes. Didn't Lenin say that?" R. replies.

"Well we capitalists actually build better bureaucracies. In the government it's one step forward, wait, one step back, wait, then two forward and one back again."

"I'm getting nauseous just listening to that. It sounds like sailing rough seas in a very small boat."

"Right! And you must learn to sail young man." Calvin says.

"I don't know. You man the sails, tacking left, tacking right, struggling all the way. But meanwhile everyone else floats along like driftwood. But the pay is the same and your boat and the driftwood wash up on shore at the same time and no one gives a shit. No one sees the difference between your boat and the driftwood."

* * * *

R. sits at his small meeting table savoring a chocolate croissant and coffee. The quiet is interrupted by hurried footsteps. *Sounds like a four-legged creature*, R. thinks.

The scurrying stops at R.'s office door as Mike and Kenny burst in causing croissant flakes to fly into the air. The pair looks as if they've lost a winning lottery ticket.

Kenny blurts out, "Hey guy. Look uh, we just got word that Franco wants to meet with you soon and discuss your program."

R. calmly brushes flakes off of his slacks and smiles as he chews, then talks with his mouth full. "Great. I'm all set," he says.

He swallows and continues, "My Strategic Plan has been ready for weeks. I was wondering when I'd have a chance to present it. There are a lot of things I want to talk with Franco about. I have ideas on how to make all of our departments more efficient, not just mine."

Kenny replies in a panic. "You don't understand. This, this is a seriously major situation of gigantic proportions."

Kenny looks over at Mike who merely strokes his goatee. Kenny goes on, "We must prepare. We have to go over your answers. Franco will ask questions. Questions! Lots of questions!"

R. says, "Of course there will be questions. I would expect nothing less. Franco is the Commissioner, basically an executive. So he'll want to know what my plans are, my budget projections, stuff like that, right?"

R. worries that Mike's chin just might catch fire from the intense stroking. Kenny's eyes go wide as he looks to Mike then back to R.

"Haven't you heard about Franco?" Kenny says.

"No, not really. What about him?" R. replies.

Kenny, nearly puking, grabs his stomach and runs out of R.'s office. Mike stops trying to ignite his chin, an action that prompts R. to consider the possibility that these clowns might be on to something.

56

Mike runs after Kenny while R. takes a final swig of coffee and treks down to Glen's office.

When he arrives, R. plops down on a black leather sofa. "So, what's the deal with Franco?" R. says.

Glen, who had been dozing, jumps and twitches as he swivels to face R.

"Franco! Shit, shut the door!" Glen yells.

Glen opens a desk drawer and pulls out a bottle of Scotch and two short glasses. He pours a healthy amount into each glass and shakily hands one to R.

"You ever wonder what would happen if Hitler and Stalin were a gay couple and adopted a son?"

"I wonder that about Dave and Aaron," R. says.

Glen ignores R. and continues. "Well Franco's that kid. He's a fucking maniac. Throws tantrums and large objects at people. Loves to terrify interns, especially the males. Don't cross him or you'll get screwed like me. Just look at this office."

R. eyes the huge office. "Seems nice to me. You've got great furniture..."

"I used to be in the Senior

Executive Service, the S-E-S! Oh those were the days. Had an office bigger than this and had Maureen, a personal secretary."

"Yeah, you've told me about her. She's useless."

"That's not the point damn it! I had a *personal* secretary. Now I'm back to being a GS-15 Director like you. No offense," Glen says.

"None taken. So you're saying I should expect the worst from this meeting with Franco? That's why Kenny and Mike are shitting their pants. He's a government executive, I mean how bad could-," R. says.

"Do you know that during one of his tantrums he literally threw a book at someone? Hit him in the head. Hard!"

R. considers asking Glen how he knew this to be true, whether this could just be an Agency legend. But as he takes a sip of Scotch he focuses on a scar just behind Glen's ear. It has always been there but at this moment it looks remarkably like…a bookmark. A bookmark from a big, hard book.

Glen continues. "Real executives try to make their organizations run more efficiently, they look to keep costs down, they make rational decisions, they motivate and inspire their employees."

Glen chugs his remaining Scotch then exclaims, "Do you see any of that happening around here?"

* * * *

The shiny elevator doors open on the sixth floor. R. steps out and proceeds leisurely towards the Agency's executive suite, Franco's lair. R. notes the relative darkness of the hall compared to the other floors.

R.'s relaxed pace is due more to the need to avoid spilling the coffee in his left hand than to a lack of nerves. He still thinks the characterizations of Franco are over the top, *But he did actually throw a book at Glen*, R. thinks.

For a while the click of R.'s shoes is the only sound in the hall. But as he hits the last stretch approaching the turn on to the 19th Street corridor he hears a familiar scurrying sound behind him. R. turns to see Kenny and Mike scrambling to catch up to him. Both are carrying bulging loose-leaf binders making any attempt at speed futile.

With Tweedle Dee and Tweedle Dum rushing towards him and the hallway that never seems to end, R. was beginning to feel a lot like Alice.

It would of course be easier if R. waited, for his boss to catch up but, *I don't really know that it's them do I, they're so far away,* R. thinks as he smiles to himself and continues walking.

Kenny eventually catches up to him and says, while panting, "Hey wait up. Why, why did you come up here alone? We stopped by your office to get you."

"I just figured we would meet in Franco's office," R. says.

"No, no, no. Franco doesn't like it when people come to him alone. And it's not really safe to be there alone anyway. There's protocol."

They continue walking together. The trio rounds the corner and R. is stunned. *It really is Wonderland,* he thinks. R. is certain that the hallway is longer than the others. The executive suite looms far off in the distance.

The décor can only be described as Nazi Nouveau. A thick, dark blue carpet covers the floor and muffles all sound. The windows are framed by long red drapes. Instead of doors, this hallway is lined with tall white columns topped with identical busts of a bald man. Who is that? R. wonders to himself.

R. stops in front of a bust and raises his right arm and says, "Heil Franco!" and smiles at Mike and Kenny who look on bewildered.

They finally cross the threshold of the waiting area. R. strides towards the executive assistant's desk which is raised high and sits in the middle of the space. R. feels like a child approaching an ice cream truck.

Mike, letting go of his goatee, grabs R. and pulls him back hissing, "Wait!" denying R. his treat.

Kenny steps forward, clears his throat, and adjusts his tie, all as if preparing to give an important speech.

"Kenny Lawrence, Executive Commissioner, reporting to see Commissioner Antonio Franco. Two guests accompanying," Kenny says.

"Please be seated. Franco is wrapping up another meeting," the assistant says.

R. and Mike walk to the waiting

area and sit on a leather sofa while Kenny approaches the assistant's desk.

"Hey, any idea what Franco's mood is today?" Kenny says.

"It's been sort of quiet so far. His Committee hearing on the Hill went well so I'd say we're at code yellow."

"Sweet. Thanks," Kenny says.

R. picks up an issue of "*Government Executive*" magazine from the glass coffee table. The headline reads "*Federal Agencies See Benefits of Embracing Efficiency*". *No one is hugging me yet*, R. laughs to himself.

As Kenny returns from the executive assistant and begins to sit shattering glass is heard coming from the direction of Franco's office, followed by heavy thumps. Then all is quiet.

Kenny jumps up, "Code red!"

They hear Franco's door open and four men dash out. Kenny follows them to the suite entrance.

"What happened in there? Should I cancel my meeting?" Kenny asks.

"Oh it's not as bad as it sounded. He only broke two things and he never took his gun out," one of the men says.

Kenny freezes with fear and only

moves when the executive assistant calls out, "The Commissioner is ready for you now, gentlemen."

Mike and R. stand up slowly as Kenny comes towards them. Then Mike and Kenny proceed side by side towards Franco's office with R. following.

They enter a large office with stately wooden furniture and red carpeting on one side and sleek, modern Euro design furniture on the other side. Franco emerges from a private bathroom on the Euro side.

R. resists the urge to salute the bald man he now recognizes from the busts in the hall.

Franco is barely Kenny's height, wears round wire frame glasses and has a slight mustache. Definitely Hitler and Mussolini's love child, R. thinks.

Franco stands in front of R. and looks him up and down, mostly up.

"You're the new one right?" Franco says.

"Yes, sir." R. says.

"Take a seat."

R. sits in the leather chair closest to him.

"Not there!" Franco shouts.

R. jumps up and moves to a different chair on the other side of a thin, sharp edged coffee table. Kenny and Mike sit ninety-degrees from R. leaving him to face Franco directly.

Franco sits and immediately turns to Mike. "Shave that fucking thing off!" he says.

Mike stops stroking the goatee but his hand remains on his face.

"Uh, shave this?"

"Yes, that! You look ridiculous and the rubbing is annoying."

"Yes, okay sir. I will shave…"

"No, I mean right fucking now! I am not sitting here looking at you stroke that thing anymore. Get the fuck out of here and shave it now!"

The instruction was certainly loud and clear but that didn't make it believable. Mike hesitates and looks over at Kenny.

Franco explodes, "You take orders from me! Not him! I command this Agency. Go shave!"

After some preliminary questions R. shows Franco some PowerPoint slides with charts and graphs. All is well until Franco begins rubbing his head with an almost Mike-like intensity.

"Stop. Just stop. I mean what is all of this?" Franco says.

64

"Well," R. begins.

"Are you trying to change things?"

"Well I'm trying to improve some things, by making changes..." R. says.

"So things are not right around here, according to you?"

"No. I mean, yes, but there's always room for improve-" R. says.

Franco turns to Kenny and shouts, "Get him out of here and explain how long it took for me to perfect things at the Agency."

Then Franco turns back to R. "As for you, you go back and develop a nice plan of how you are not going to change one fucking thing!"

* * * *

R. reads a magazine as the Metro travels on above ground tracks. Despite the air conditioning he is toasting due to the sun beating down through the windows. The subway car is nearly full but there's an empty seat next to him.

The train crawls into the Arlington Cemetery station, giving the hordes of waiting tourists on the platform time to realize they should perhaps not lean their heads into the

65

path of an oncoming train.

The doors open and the tourists pile in. Calvin and other regular commuters are among them. Calvin notices R. and approaches the empty seat.

Calvin puts on a wholesome Midwestern accent. "Excuse me sir, I'm sorry to bother you, may I sit here next to you?"

R. remains buried in his magazine. He simply nods and says, "Sure. Go ahead."

Calvin sits and continues his role as tourist. "Gosh, so many people are reading. Do you read everyday on your way to work? It's a really good habit."

R. looks up slightly and turns just enough to see Calvin and laughs.

"You know a tourist actually asked me that once." R. says.

"Me too! And when they see *me* with a Kindle it's 'I guess older people in the big cities keep up with technology'. Bastards!" Calvin says.

"So why are you getting on from the Cemetery station anyway?"

"Look at my hair. Don't you know we older people live in coffins? No, the train I was on had a sick passenger and off-loaded at the Cemetery."

"I'll never figure out why they don't take the sick passenger off the train and let the rest of us get on with our lives."

"Ha. First you brush off a good-natured tourist and now you're speaking ill of the ill. It's only 9:30. You can't be in a shitty mood already."

"I met Franco yesterday." R. says.

"Touché," Calvin says then adding, "I remember when that little asshole started at the Agency."

R. replies, "And you've had the privilege of watching him move up the ranks past you. See I just don't get that, how do you put up with that?"

"Yes, he passed me but that was years ago. Now we are level. You can't lose sight of the big picture. Let time do its thing."

"I'm trying not to lose my soul as this time thing you talk about ticks by. I've seen so many smart, dedicated people but they've given up. Who can blame them when idiots like Kenny and Mike rise to the top? I don't want that to happen to me. I don't want to give up, fade away and collect a check. The whole point of me joining government was to help bring about positive changes, in whatever small way I can. What's your secret Calvin?"

"Well..." Calvin begins but the subway car enters the Rosslyn tunnel and R. can't hear a thing.

* * * *

The news plays on the radio as R. eats a bowl of oatmeal at his kitchen table. It's been a while since he's had breakfast at home.

He begins to clean up when he hears a reporter say, "...*today is the first day in decades that federal employees will have to pay for their own Metro commute. Due to a law signed last year, the Metro transit subsidy for federal employees has been eliminated. The President says the government will save fifty million dollars per year. But there is widespread concern that government workers won't show up to work today...*"

"What kind of people wouldn't show up? Who else besides federal employees gets paid to commute?" R. says to the radio.

Later R. rides a nearly empty Metro to work. He begins to wonder if it's Friday. He arrives at the Agency and finds it a ghost town. Oddly none of the guards advises him to go home.

The quiet is a bit eerie at first but he settles in and takes advantage of the fact that there's no one around to interrupt him.

"Oh, you're here," Darcy says, coming from out of nowhere.

R. jumps a bit and says, "Why wouldn't I be here?"

"Well, I don't know. Maybe you would stay away, to show solidarity with your federal comrades who make less than you and are hit by the Metro subsidy cut."

Darcy succeeds in getting a rise out of R.

"Is that why no one is here? No wonder Mike and Aaron act like free coffee is a right. Hell, why not? Taxpayers pay for everything else."

"Free coffee?" Darcy says.

"Nothing, just some nonsense. But seriously, who, outside this crazy government bubble, gets paid by their company to commute to their own job?" R. says.

Darcy's silence concedes the point.

R. says, "If you're so adversely affected, why are you here?"

Darcy smiles. "I have work to do. It's not a foreign concept to all of us feds."

R. laughs but it doesn't last long. He realizes that he is obligated by law to verify the whereabouts of his other staff who, technically, are AWOL. So his day starts with uncomfortable, intolerable phone calls:

"Monique, I know you have a long commute. But that's not new...right, right I know. Right, it is a new expense but...right, right, but think of it this way, you and millions of other federal employees are joining the rest of the country. Now, come on, it's not robbery. Look, how long are you going to stay away? I really don't think it will take a year to raise commuting funds. Maybe cut back on lunch or something...no, no I'm not saying you eat too much..Monique, Monique, you know I..Monique? Monique?"

"Yes, this is Dave. Oh, hi, boss. Yeah, you know this Metro subsidy thing is rough. I don't know how I'm going to make it to work again...well, you make that sound

easy but..but this is not just about money, it's principle..this pay my own way to work stuff doesn't seem fair. Next they'll be linking raises to performance. Hey, don't worry, boss, I'm just taking some Unexpected Duress Leave. I think I only have about 15 days of it stored up..yes, I understand. I will try..yeah, okay. Thanks, boss."

"Aaron here..No, boss, I'm not sick. You know perfectly well why I'm not there..oh, are you calling me a slave? Yes, I know I took a civil servant's oath but I have rights. I thought about coming in today you know..yeah, I did. I thought about it, and you know what I started thinking? I realized this was my opportunity. My opportunity to get the name of my department changed..right, maybe I won't come in unless you give proper consideration to changing the name of my department..Well, yeah, I guess you can say I'm on strike..but are you going to think about the name..no, boss, I don't see this as a form of extortion..."

Eventually R. is able to remove the Bluetooth earpiece from his numb ears. He leans back in his chair and considers going to Glen's office for some Scotch but settles for a glass of Bordeaux simply because he has a

71

bottle in his own desk drawer.

R. twirls his glass and sips the wine as he considers that he has in fact achieved something today. He has managed to ensure that most, if not all, of his staff will return soon, 'soon' in government time.

He takes another sip of wine as he ponders the return of Aaron and Dave. "Definitely need the Scotch," R. says as he gets up and heads to Glen's office.

* * * *

R. has been trying to hire additional staff for weeks and he's insisted on finding people from outside of the Agency.

Franco, despite his tantrum actually approved R.'s staff increase request. A sadist wouldn't turn down new victims, R. figures.

R. enlisted the HR Department's help in sending out the job notices. They've just let him know that enough applications have arrived to begin a review.

The HR Department's office area is undoubtedly the worst in the entire building. An elevator takes R. to the basement and the door opens up to a hall with low ceilings and flickering fluorescent lights.

Stooping slightly R. walks gingerly through a passage that leads to a row of tattered cubicles. Finally he finds Tania, his HR rep's desk.

She's not there but he notices a few résumés lying on her desk and sees college names like Northwestern, Duke, and the University of Michigan.

Tania enters the passageway and comes to her desk and sees R. waiting. "Oh, hey. I'm glad you came down 'cause I need to tell you that these applicants ain't qualified enough," she says.

"Not qualified enough? You have heard of these schools, right?" R. says.

"No. And that don't matter no ways. They don't meet the requirements. For instance there ain't nothing in their résumés saying they gots writing skills," Tania says.

"They have Master's degrees in policy analysis from some of the best schools in the nation. I think they can write. The degrees speak for themselves," R. says.

"It doesn't say 'Masters in Writing'." R. tries to chime in but

Tania continues, "It doesn't say 'Masters in Analytical Skills.'"

"No, no," R. pleads. "I mean that in order to get into, much less graduate from, these schools, a person obviously—"

"I can't go by what's obvious. I can only go by what I see," Tania says.

"Have you ever considered working at the security desk?"

Later Calvin and R. chat while standing in a crowded Metro car. The train is stopped at a station and passengers are squeezing in. The conductor begins shouting interrupts their conversation, "Step all the way in please! Step all the way in! Move to the center of the car."

Calvin and R. inch a bit further into the car and hold on to a pole. The train begins to move, jerking forward then slamming to a halt again.

Amidst the din of apologies for stepped on toes and knocked shoulders, R. and Calvin manage to continue their conversation.

"I've managed to get smart people onboard. But it is hard. Next time don't list a bunch of skills you are looking for, just give HR the list of schools you want people from. And you don't do that until after you've already found the candidates you want. The HR people are just drones. Program them right and they'll do what you want," Calvin says.

"This lady Jennifer Schmitt said she and her team could help me." R. says.

"Jennifer can't spell 'help'."

"What? She's no good?"

"Useless. But if you have a meeting set up already don't cancel it. You'll never get rid of her, she's worse than a Jehovah's Witness on a Saturday morning. The existence of her division, and her job, depends on the number of other divisions she helps. The meeting is her version of 'helping'. She has to make quota."

The following week Darcy and R. rush into the all-white Architect's conference room. "Sorry we're late," R. says.

Jennifer and her entire staff are seated around the table. Jennifer is a middle aged, earnest, mid-western woman with a sunny disposition.

"Oh, no problem at all. It's been lovely just sitting in this room," Jennifer says. "These plants are lovely."

Darcy takes an empty seat next to Jennifer and R. sits across from her.

"Well, thanks so much for offering to help me. I didn't know your department even existed," R says.

"Oh absolutely, our pleasure. It's hard to know who we are because we're so integrated with the Agency. We're like an octopus with eight helping hands spread out for everyone," Jennifer says as she stretches her arms out and shakes them around to illustrate the octopus. Darcy grimaces as she ducks for cover.

R. says, "Well again I appreciate it. As we discussed when we first met I've been having a very hard time getting new people hired on at the Agency..."

"Have you tried Human Resources?" Jennifer says.

R. raises his eyebrows and exchanges a confused look with Darcy then replies to Jennifer. "Uh yes, of course, but..."

"Hmm well that's a big step.

They really are the group to go to for this sort of thing." Jennifer says.

"Yes, right, but HR has not really been as helpful as we'd like and I thought, and you said, your team could help get around-" R. says.

"Oh absolutely. We will definitely help. That's what we do."

"So you understand that HR is my problem."

"Hmm, have you thought about trying the Department of Labor?"

Darcy diverts a laugh explosion back down into her body that convulses as she pretends to cough.

R. manages to utter, "Uh..the Department of Labor is not really..."

"Oh but they do have a lot to do with workers, workers all across the country. They have these wonderful centers for poor people, nice brown people like yourself, to go and find work, and..."

R. gets a strange tingling sensation on his head that he's dying to rub and finds himself valiantly resisting the urge to throw a book.

"Look, wait. Wait a minute. Okay. Fine. We'll try the Department of Labor. Will you and your team reach out to contacts there?" R. says.

"Oh absolutely. We would love to help, that's what we do. We play an advisory role. We give guidance." Jennifer says.

"Ah, and you are guiding me to the Department of Labor for hiring."

"Right. And I'm sure we'll come up with some other resources to point you to."

"I thought you were the resource."

"Oh absolutely. We are. We point you..."

"So you are not really eight arms. You're more like little fingers." R. says.

R. raises his hands and points both index fingers and shakes them around.

"Hmm well, uhm I never really thought of it... gosh, that might be a good way to describe..." Jennifer begins.

"Oh, but wait. You don't use these fingers, you use these," R. says as he substitutes his middle fingers for the index fingers. He continues, "Because anyone that actually thinks you can help with anything is fucked!"

R. slams his chair back as he gets up and storms out of the room. *At*

least F-bombs leave no visible scars,
he thinks.

Jennifer turns and smiles at Darcy. "Is he angry with us? I thought we were very helpful."

"Oh absolutely." Darcy says.

* * * *

R. wakes in his office chair. His blinds are closed so it seems late and he feels as if he's been asleep for ages. He checks his phone and it is only 3:45 p.m.

Taking advantage of the relative calm, he opens a PowerPoint presentation that he's been working on for the Vegas Conference. He manages to revise five slides before he hears sheep. At first he thinks it is someone's ring tone but no one else is around. Then he hears footsteps approaching, many of them. Both sounds become louder and definitely closer.

R. opens his office door and looks out into the corridor. A herd of sheep stream by heading to the rear exit stairs. He looks upstream and sees Uncle Sam striding among the herd holding a shepherd's crook. He also notices that the sheep have the faces of Agency employees.

R. slams his door shut and stands with his back against it, his heart racing. A hard knock sends vibrations through the door and his body. R. doesn't dare open the door.

"Come on," Uncle Sam's voice booms. "Stop wasting your time. Join me."

R. doesn't respond and quiet returns to the hall. Then he hears the sheep bleating outside. He walks away from the door slowly and opens one of the windows.

Looking down he sees Uncle Sam still leading the herd. Uncle Sam looks up, points at R. and says, "It's four o'clock. Time to go."

R. shouts, "I have work to do!"

At this Uncle Sam stops pointing and holds up his middle finger. The sheep look up at R. and say, "Baaah!"

At this, R. wakes with a shudder, the back of his shirt soaked with sweat. The Uncle Sam hallucinations are morphing into full-blown nightmares. *Maybe the sheep are right, I am working too much. I'll just book my Vegas flights then get out of here*, he thinks.

On the government travel booking system all tickets to Vegas are

$1,400. These are supposedly special government-negotiated rates but R. searches Expedia and finds $800 tickets and buys them. *I just saved $600 bucks, wonder if anyone will even care.*

Travel Daze

A blast of heat from the Las Vegas oven welcomes R. as he steps from the plane onto the jet way. Seconds later he enters the Antarctic terminal.

As he walks down the busy concourse he sees passengers at another gate, arriving from Washington. It's surely filled with people he does not want to meet right now so he speeds up.

He makes it unscathed to the escalators leading to ground transportation but then, "Hey, hey!" Brett's voice booms as he catches up to R.

"Have a good flight?" Brett says. "That sure was a good days' work."

"What do you mean? It's only 10:00. The day is just beginning." R. says.

"You really need to catch up on your government procedures. It's ten here but one o'clock at home."

"Well, okay, so we have a half

day left."

"Half! No sir. I don't know about you but I recall getting to the airport at five a.m. to make my flight. The rules say our day begins at that moment. So it's been eight hours, my friend. Day over. And anything we do today is overtime. Why do you think the Big Agency Conference is always held on the West Coast? We get playtime!"

R. lets Brett's wisdom sink in as they wait in the long taxi line. He wanted to Uber but decided not to complicate things by doing something simple and more efficient.

They eventually arrive at the swanky V Resort Spa & Casino. The gentle pulsing beats of electronic dance music mix with the sound of slot machines. Everything possible has been done to create a Miami in the desert.

Brett takes in the scenery. "Can you believe it? For one week this place is going to be a federal paradise," he says.

"And apparently with ample opportunity to have paradise lost," R. says.

After checking in they head to their respective rooms. The first item on the agenda is Kenny's Happy Hour meeting at 1:00pm, brilliantly timed to coincide with Washington Happy Hour time.

R.'s appointment notes indicate that "appropriate attire" is requested for the "pool-side" meeting. *As if there's anything appropriate about a pool-side office meeting,* R. thinks.

When R. arrives for the meeting he is awed by the lush palm trees, bright blue pools, and the horde of government interns in thong bikinis sunning themselves or slithering amongst senior officials.

R. looks around and sees his fellow directors grouped at one end of a serpentine pool submerged up to their chests. As R. tries to process the scene his back is stung by the thick, wet jelly-fish hands of Kenny.

"Hey dude!" Kenny says. "Come on get your drink and jump in. I'm about to make my entrance and get the party...uh, meeting started."

For once R. considers Kenny the source of wisdom. A drink is indeed a very good idea. And with this thought barely complete, an intern, whose thong happens to be R.'s favorite color, gently takes him by the hand,

"I'll escort you to the bar sir."

R. and his betrothed stroll to the poolside bar. He orders his usual Grey Goose on the rocks with a twist of lime but makes it a double. He thanks the intern for her service and she assures him that it was her pleasure.

R. decides to savor his first drink at the bar while he's alone, then take another to the pool meeting.

As he sips he takes in more of the scene, this time noting the hot tubs and cabanas. Then another escort approaches with Malcolm on her arm. Malcolm is a well-known and very good looking director who has the benefit of not working for Kenny. R. overhears Malcolm chatting up the intern, *or is it mentoring*, R. thinks.

"You can't go wrong hooking up with a government man," Malcolm is saying. "Better than a Wall Street guy, we all know who had to bail them out, right? Yep, the government men."

R. stifles a laugh. It was an amazing blend of insightfulness and bullshit.

Malcolm continues, "A Wall Street guy may have big dollars today, maybe tomorrow too, but the next day, who knows? But a government man like me, I have my six figures and I'm *guaranteed* those six figures, *forever.* And you know what else I have? Benefits! Big benefits!"

R. half expects Malcolm to pull a benefit out of his pants but he merely offers the intern his hand and gives her his card.

R. figures he should finally get to the meeting so he orders his second drink and walks towards the pool. He felt naked without an intern on his arm, *strange how you can get used to malfeasance,* R. thinks.

A chorus of "come on in" greets R. as he approaches the pool. The men are all in high spirits but the female directors are a vision of despair. Most are standing cross-armed and it's not because they are cold. The women received a version of Kenny's "appropriate attire" instructions that were a bit different than what R. received.

Seeing their condition angers R. but he was honestly too buzzed to respond rationally or even display a hint of sympathy. He steps into the pool and wades to join the others. As he settles in and places his drink on the edge of the pool he is joined, of course, by the same intern who escorted him earlier. R. began to wonder whether she really was a government intern or an actual escort, *I mean how many gorgeous interns could we possibly have? And we are in Vegas...* R. thinks.

A loud gong interrupts his thoughts. Without any warning Kenny comes charging and screaming out of a cabana and does a massive belly flop in the pool.

The splash forces everyone to turn away and raise their arms, hence the female directors are forced to reveal their appropriate attire.

"Whoooo hooo!" Kenny yells. "Did ya see that? Man!"

Kenny makes his way to the head of the pool while an intern hands him a drink. He takes a sip and says, "Goooood Afternoooon Las Vegas!"

He apparently expects a rousing response and is disappointed. "Come on guys, perk up. Isn't this sweet? Pool-side meeting! Glad you could all make it and glad you all came dressed appropriately."

Kenny laughs but then becomes serious as he points at Deena. "Deena,

I have to apologize on your behalf. My secretary made a mistake and sent you the wrong instructions. None of us wanted to see you like this, really. Sorry, my bad. But hey, somebody is coming with a big robe you can wear, okay? Cool. Okay, now let's get to work. Commissioner Franco is ready to start."

The directors look around. There had been no sign of Franco at all and no one relished the idea of being in a pool when he showed up.

The wait is short. Franco, a Napoleon in swim trunks, emerges from the steam of a nearby hot tub and walks over to the pool. He stands, legs apart, directly over Kenny's head as water drips from his trunks. Kenny remains in place as if he's a helpless man caught in a summer downpour without an umbrella.

"Good afternoon everyone. Thanks for coming," Franco begins. "As you know the Agency has struggled to provide good customer service over the years. That's why I've convened this task force to tackle the problem head on."

R. listens but can't take his eyes off of the Franco-Kenny baptism.

In addition to water, sweat rolls down from Franco's head and makes it's way on to Kenny, each drop taking a literal nose dive.

Franco continues, "This is a critical mission. I expect you to be bold. We need your ideas. Don't hold back, don't be afraid to propose radical changes."

The directors in the pool look at each other warily, each having their own flashbacks to Franco's reaction to past 'bold' proposals:

"Did you just tell me what you think! Who asked you to think? You direct, I think for you!"

"You can come back and lay out your nice plan for how you are not going to change one fucking thing!"

"You want our agency to be the first to implement this? We're not paying you to innovate! Just do your fucking job!"

The directors merely nod their acknowledgement of Franco's words with absolutely no intent of following up with action. *This is how they survive,* R. thinks.

"So, get started ladies and gentlemen. You are the leaders. I'm expecting great things from you,"

Franco says.

Franco turns around and disappears once again into the steam. Kenny hoists himself up on to the edge of the pool and an intern dabs him with a towel.

"Okay everybody. You heard Franco. Let's get started. Let's brainstorm and get some good ideas going. How are we going to tackle our customer service problem?" he says.

R., not sufficiently buzzed to kill his common sense says, "Actually I think this will be easier than it sounds. When my staff was cleaning up for the Move they came across some old Client Service Improvement Initiative documents from 2009."

Light splashes of recognition came from the other directors as they murmured, "I remember that."

R. continues, "So we have a chance to actually implement the things figured out in 2009. It would be a shame for all of that hard work to go to waste." The other directors nod in agreement.

Kenny says, "Wellll, we want to be careful. We can't just copy everything from before."

"It's not copying, this stuff

was never done." R. says.

"Right, but we have to make sure we develop up to date approaches. The only way to do that is to brainstorm and *that* means we'll need at least three more off-site meetings. So we have to start looking into some good locations to hold those brainstorming meetings."

R.'s effect on the other directors wears off at Kenny's mention of 'good locations'. He looks around at their surroundings, the palms, the pools, and the booze. Even the forcibly appropriately dressed female directors can't resist. The thought of more working vacations like this one casts a spell on all of them.

Nevertheless R. persisted, "But why are we starting at the beginning when so much has already been figured out? Don't you think it's time to…,"

"Oh it is, but we have to schedule the meetings. You've raised a good point, we'll definitely put it on the agenda," Kenny says. He then addresses the group, "So, where are we gonna have that first brainstorm? Miami? That sound good?"

R. takes a deep breath and submerges himself. He sits on the bottom of the pool and enjoys the silence.

* * * *

"Please be back in twenty minutes," the instructor announces. The first half of a very long mandatory training session was over. R. had been late thanks to a useless morning meeting. Darcy had saved a seat for him in the huge ballroom. Through most of the session they'd taken turns nudging each other when one nodded off. Their system failed at some point because this time the announcement was the nudge waking them both.

They leave the room and enter the vast Las Vegas Convention Center halls. R., a bit desperate, asks, "Where are the bathrooms around here?"

Darcy gives him a look and answers, "I think they're down on the north end."

"Did I hear *you* say 'north'? Studying geography finally?"

"No, I'm too busy tutoring you in reading", Darcy replies as she points to a large sign that reads RESTROOMS, NORTH END.

When R. returns from the north,

he and Darcy decide to check out the rest of the convention center. They round a corner to a semi-secluded hallway. Outside one of the rooms a sign propped on an easel reads, FEDERAL CONSULTING STRATEGY–BREAK OUT SESSION.

As they approach the door R.'s former boss from his old consulting firm steps out

"Hey! Wow, good to see you. I was wondering if you'd be here," she says.

"Well, here I am working and sinning on your dime," R. says. "What are *you* doing in Vegas, Michelle?"

"Federal business," Michelle says.

"What? The firm is doing government work now?"

"Oh, it's a long story, but yes we are. Look, I can tell you all about it over dinner tonight if you're free."

"Sure, that would be great," R. says.

"Okay, good. Let's do Jaleo at seven thirty. I know how much you love the one in D.C."

"It's a date then. Can I bring my partner in crime?" R. says as he motions to Darcy. "I'm trying to save her the agony of dining with highly paid feds who insist on eating at McDonald's."

"Of course she can come. I have plenty of dirt to give her on her boss," Michelle says with a laugh.

That evening Darcy, Michelle, and R. lean back in their plush multi-colored seats and have a lively conversation as plates of Spanish tapas are cleared away and simultaneously replaced with more.

"So what's got the firm so interested in public service," R. says to Michelle before taking another sip of a fantastic Rioja. "What was it you said to me when I said I was leaving the firm and going to the government? Oh yeah, something like 'paying taxes is enough of a contribution to society'," R. says.

"Very funny," Michelle says. "Look I still think you're nuts to actually go *in* to the government but I've spoken to some of the usual government consultants and it's insane the money they make from Uncle Sam."

R., who hasn't 'seen' Uncle Sam in a while, looks around a bit nervously at the mention of his name.

"What's wrong?" Darcy says.

"Oh, nothing. Just seeing who can hear us."

Michelle continues, "I actually sat in on a meeting where four firms were planning their 'Spin Cycle'. One firm gets hired to do an organizational efficiency analysis of an agency, they *always* recommend a reorganization. Then the second firm is hired to advise the agency on the reorganization. Of course the advice is bogus and everything becomes a mess so the third firm is hired to implement some software solution. The software makes everything worse so the agency pays the firm to train all of the agency's employees. At this point at least five years have gone by and the agency is convinced that it needs to assess the efficiency of it's operations, so it's back to square one, the cycle continues."

"And our firm, I mean, your firm wants in on this larceny," R. says.

"Hell yes! We're talking hundreds of millions of dollars. We never make that kind of money so easily with private sector clients. They wouldn't fall for this bullshit."

Michelle continues, "We can even make money by screwing up on purpose. Bad software equals more 'bug fixes', bad 'bug fixes, equals more training. And shit, training can go on forever!"

"And you have no qualms about this Michelle?" Darcy asks.

"No. Look it's *The Lion King.* Circle of Life shit. It's how we survive. We keep people employed, the feds keep people employed. It all works out."

* * * *

Uncle Sam is slumped over a large wooden desk filled with papers in an ornate room. His hat lays on the floor among another messy pile of papers. With the hat off, his long white hair hangs down flat. He struggles to hold a pen in his hands as four consultants surround him, two on either side, each from a different firm. Upon closer inspection one can see that the papers are all contracts. Uncle Sam has been signing hundreds of them all night.

Sweat pours down Uncle Sam's face. He's exhausted and feels lucky to have so much help. It's difficult to spend trillions of dollars without advice. In front of his desk stand another four consultants. Two more are under the desk massaging his feet. Another begins to comb his hair and pat the sweaty icon's head with a small handkerchief.

Meanwhile Uncle Sam continues his labor. He carefully rolls up each contract, ties it with silk ribbon and hands them to the winning firm.

R.'s alarm rescues him from yet another nightmare. *Yeah Michelle, it all works out,* he thinks to himself.

Thanks to the dream R. feels dirty enough for an extra long shower. After dressing he sprints down to the hotel lounge where Kenny is holding a mandatory breakfast meeting.

The nightclub buzz of the lounge has been replaced by a gentle spa-like hum. R. is the last Director to arrive but Kenny has yet to appear. As he finds a space to sit he is surprised to see Kirkland until he remembers that the hotel has tofu eggs and other foods alien to Kenny.

The Directors, seated on leather ottomans around a large table under a huge chandelier, chat amongst themselves until Mike and Kenny finally step out of an elevator and approach. Behind them is a short man who seems to be walking on his tip-toes, willing himself to be tall.

Kenny gives R. a "hey, guy" as he steps among the seats. Then, to everyone, he says, "Hey, listen up. Please, everybody rise. We have a very important guest this morning. He's the man who made this conference possible. The awesome food, this sweet hotel, all of it. I can't tell you how many times I've sat with this man to discuss my future. He showed me the ropes and now here I am, an Executive Commissioner.

"He has graciously agreed to meet with us this morning, taking time from his very busy schedule, to show us how our Office can survive these budget cuts. So now please bow your heads and avert your gaze as Mr. Jeb Stanly honors us with his presence."

The Directors each bow their heads. Kenny and Mike make the sign of the cross.

Stanly enters the lounge slowly, nodding from side to side. Then he raises his arms and says, "You may now be seated."

Everyone sits. After a moment of reverent silence, Stanly speaks.

"My dear colleagues, the current president has, hell, every damned president, has told us we need to cut costs, cut staff, cut our budgets. Cut, cut, cut! I know all of you on Kenny's team are worried about your programs. Well I'm here today to teach you a thing or two about cutting.

"The first thing you need to do is understand what kind of animal the government is. You see everyone talks about government being an unwieldy beast. They're wrong. The government, my friends, is nothing but a starfish."

Stanly reaches into his suit jacket and pulls out a live starfish, which he slaps down on the table. Then he pulls out a knife.

"You can cut this baby all you want, but it's gonna grow back!"

Fortunately not too many other live creatures are butchered the rest of the day. Six hours go by as Kenny and his Directors, with the help of Jeb Stanly and a few Bloody Marys, devise a strategy that will help them all keep eighty percent of their budget while making it look like fifty percent was cut. R. is sick in his soul but he can't help but admire

99

Stanly's ingenuity.

* * * *

"I hear they're unveiling the
new travel software," Brett says to R.
as they ride the escalator down to the
conference ballroom.

They weed their way through a
thicket of scantily clad interns and
enter the ballroom.

"Wow, is this the Consumer
Electronics Conference or something?"
R. says as he observes the slick
tables, funky chairs, showroom cars,
balloons, ultra-modern lights, roving
jugglers, and mounds of food.

"Welcome to Vegas!" an intern
squeals as R. simultaneously feels a
squeeze on his ass. Eager to avoid
blackmail, R. walks away briskly to
one of the bars where he finds Darcy.

"You want a drink?" R. asks.

"Sure, I'll drink with you so
you won't be drinking alone," Darcy
replies.

"Oh, I won't be alone. It's an
open bar."

"No way!"

"Yeah, and after my meeting
today I know not to ask how Jeb Stanly
pulled this off. Today's fraud quota

has definitely been reached."

"What?"

"Oh, nothing. Nothing," R. says.

They take their drinks and sit at a large circular table draped in blue and white. The lights dim and a spotlight appears on the stage. A booming voice announces in heavyweight boxing style, "And now, ladies and gentlemen, please rise for the Wise Wizard of the West Region, Jehhhhb Stanleee!"

Balloons are released, bubbles erupt from places unknown, champagne bottles pop, confetti rains down, and the audience cheers wildly. Stanly walks into the spotlight, waving and bowing at the adoring crowd. After ten minutes calm is restored.

"I'm so glad all of you could make it out here tonight. This year's gala...uhm conference is going to be a blast. Bigger and better than any we've done before.

"To start things off, I thought tonight would be the perfect time to reveal the Agency's brand new travel reservation software."

The crowd erupts with applause.

Stanly continues, "You know, in these times where everyone is out to cut our budgets..."

At this, a chorus of *boos* sounds.

"Yes, yes, I know, I know. In times like these we always get stronger, right?"

The crowd echoes, "Right!"

"Well it took nearly all of my strength but here we are in Vegas, ready to work..."

The crowd boos, then Stanly adds, "...and ready to party!"

At this point, rock-concert euphoria sweeps across the ballroom. It takes a full three minutes for the crowd to settle down.

"So let's kick things off. Ladies and gentlemen, I am pleased to introduce Kevin Powers, CEO of CFI Incorporated!"

The crowd, which by now will cheer at anything, cheers loudly while Powers walks on stage wearing slick blue jeans and a black turtleneck.

"Thank you. Thank you. Oh, gosh. Thanks. And thanks, Jeb, for that introduction. Now I just want to mention something that I'm sure Jeb is too modest to say himself. If it weren't for him, this twenty million dollar, mind-blowing software I'm about to unveil would not have been possible. So on behalf of myself, my children, my church, CFI employees, and CFI shareholders, thank *you*, Jeb Stanly!"

The crowd erupts again. Eventually Powers is able to continue.

"At CFI we know you hate clunky software. Government workers are world travelers who deserve the most sophisticated tools. Booking your next trip should not be a hassle." Powers pauses for effect and then says, "And it won't be!"

The crowd explodes.

"It won't be a hassle because your next trip will be booked using a revolutionary system that we call…GovGo."

A GovGo logo appears on screens hanging on all sides of the ballroom. Michael Jackson's "Thriller" plays in the background while the audience goes orgasmic.

Kevin Powers, now shouting, continues, "So let's Go! Gov! Are you planning to attend a mandatory training session in Honolulu? No problem. Just go to GovGo dot gov!"

At this, the screen shows the site's homepage. Darcy leans over to

R. and says, "Isn't that the Orbitz site?"

"I was thinking Expedia," R. says. "It could be any of those."

While R. and Darcy compare thoughts, Powers walks the crowd through the software features. "...So after you enter that information, voila! Up comes a list of flights..."

R. exclaims, "Twenty million dollars was spent on this? It's Expedia with a different cover. It's like those PowerPoint presentations we saw. New cover, same contents."

"I know," Darcy says hoping to calm R. She's never seen him this worked up.

"Expedia is free," R. says. "It's free!"

"Shh. I know. I know," Darcy says.

"This is bullshit!"

"I know. Shh!"

A voice from the audience shouts out, "Will there be training for this?"

Powers smiles and responds. "Training? Oh, absolutely. Once again, thank Jeb. He found an additional five million dollars to provide training for everyone. We know it can take a while to get used to something so new."

At this, R. leaps out of his seat and shrieks, "New?!"

Darcy has visions of the Gestapo dragging her boss out of the hall. But instead R.'s outburst only fans the flames of the crowds frenzy. Groups jump up chanting, "New! New! New!"

Darcy grabs R.'s hand and yells, "Let's get out of here."

The softness of Darcy's hands soothes R.'s seething blood but it's her vice grip and uncanny 5'3" strength that gets him out of the ballroom.

Together they exit the convention center's Arctic environs and reacquaint themselves with the desert heat. They decide to walk the two miles back to the hotel figuring it will help R. calm down. Besides, it's a beautiful night.

Daze End

Their flight is nearly over. R. looks down at what must be West Virginia. Next to him, Darcy is saying, "Are you sure you're ready to go through with it?"

"I have to, who else will?" R. says.

"Our hero!" Darcy laughs.

R. laughs as he stands and says, "Well if you'll pardon me, your hero must go perform a mortal function."

He steps into the narrow aisle and walks to the front restroom. Inside, he leans his head against the sloped ceiling as he pees.

After flushing the toilet R. turns to the sink, washes his hands, and splashes some water on his face. When he looks up into the mirror he jumps and lets out a short scream. He sees and feels Uncle Sam standing behind him.

For a second R. manages a humorous thought, noting how amazing it is that Uncle Sam can fit in an airplane bathroom even with his hat on. The humor fades when his thoughts switch to the reality of being dry-humped by a 240-year-old white guy.

R. manages to squirm and twist himself around. Uncle Sam is not in a good mood. He stares sharply into R.'s eyes, points a long, scraggly index finger in his face, and says with tobacco-scented breath, "I Want You. To Ctuop! Don't morr with the Government."

Despite having just relieved himself R. is certain that he's wet his pants. He tries to wriggle free but Uncle Sam grabs his throat.

"When you sit back down you remember to SHUT UP!"

Uncle Sam loosens his grip slightly.

"Everything will be all right. Just SHUT UP and you'll keep MOVING UP. Nice and easy. No need to change a thing."

* * * *

Darcy gives R. a hug in the Agency lobby, "Good luck."

As Darcy goes to the elevators, R. opens a large, heavy door marked, OFFICE OF THE INSPECTOR GENERAL.

The door closes behind R. with a

loud click. He walks down a dim, narrow corridor and passes a small cluttered room as he heads to the Inspector General's office. A woman comes out of the room.

"The Inspector is not in his office at the moment. He has a slight cold," she says.

"Sorry to hear that. Can I reschedule?"

"Oh, no need. The Inspector will see you today. He'll just receive you in bed."

The woman leads R. down another corridor and they come to a large brown door. She knocks twice before entering.

The room is dark and musty with a huge bed in the middle. R., hears a phlegmatic voice call out, "Please come in. Come around to my left side. Then you can tell me what's troubling you."

The light coming through a single tall window illuminates the Inspector and the bed.

R. walks to the far side of the bed.

"Now make yourself comfortable, have a seat," the Inspector says.

R. looks around for a place to

sit but sees nothing. Then, like a ghost, Uncle Sam emerges from a dark corner carrying a chair. With a sinister grin he says to R., "Yes. Please, do have a seat."

Last Friday

R. springs up in his low-lying bed breathing heavily. He shakes his head thinking, *Maybe today these nightmares will end.*

R. gets out of bed and dresses quickly. He wants to make it to the bar in time to watch the congressional hearings. He's pretty sure nearly everyone at the Agency will be crammed in at the Exchequer, the filthy bar everyone seems to love.

When he arrives downtown R. buys a baguette, he'll need it today to soak up the morning's alcohol.

As predicted the Exchequer is packed. The televisions are all tuned to C-Span. R. edges his way through the crowd and finds Darcy, Calvin, Brett, and Monique.

Calvin shakes hands with R. "Nice work sir. Very nice," he says.

Before R. can respond the televisions are un-muted and the banging of a gavel brings a hush to the crowd.

On screen, Kenny, Stanly, and

110

Franco stand side by side behind a long table holding up their right hands. A panel of Congressmen sits across from them in raised seats.

The three each solemnly swear to tell the truth and the questions begin.

Franco leans over the table in order to reach the microphone "Mr. Chairman, on the advice of counsel, I respectfully decline to answer based upon my Fifth Amendment constitutional privilege."

A Congressman asks Kenny, "Were you aware that excess money was spent at that conference? Significant excess? Did you see the plans for this conference?"

A dumbstruck Kenny replies, "I, uh, think, there was a PowerPoint slide deck... but I did not see it."

"So it was not important enough for you to see?"

Another Congressman cuts in, "You know, as I walked around my district this weekend, a lot of people were complaining about having to pay the IRS. Yet at this conference, Agency employees stayed in luxury suites, charged expenses for after-hour parties, expensive drinks..."

This goes on for quite some time. Eventually the Agency's Inspector General takes the oath and prepares to answer questions. R. and Darcy let out a "Whoop!"

"Is it true that during your investigation witnesses told you they were scared that Mr. Franco would retaliate against them if they blew the whistle?" the Congressman asks.

"Yes. Yes sir. And not just Franco. Jeb Stanly also threatened to squash employees like a bug if they spoke up." The IG says.

At this, one Congressman loses it, "Mr. Stanly, you know, as I look through this, there is no wonder that the American people have lost faith in their government.

"And I got to tell you, it is so easy to spend somebody else's money. I think it is absolutely ridiculous that the American people have to sit back and watch this.

"Mr. Stanly, do you think it is your money?"

"I do think it is my money. I am a taxpayer..." Stanly says.

"Excuse me? Did you say you think it's your money?"

"Well, I do pay taxes..."

"So the $8,000 spent on skimpy intern outfits was okay?"

The Congressman turns to Kenny. "Do you think it is your money?"

R. laughs and yells at the television, "Come on Kenny, you can get this one right!"

"No. I believe it is the taxpayers' money." Kenny replies to the Congressman.

The crowd at the Exchequer cheers.

"Mr. Franco, let's see if you'll answer this one. Do you think the $1 million spent in Vegas was your money?"

"I believe it is the taxpayers' money," Franco says.

"Okay, let's try again Mr. Stanly. Do you think the $130,000 spent on balloons, condoms, and champagne was your money?"

"I believe that money belongs to the taxpayers." Stanly says.

"The part that galls me the most is the hypocrisy of the Agency not even following its own damn rules. You are so quick to make everyone else follow the rules, and you can't follow your own rules," one exasperated Congressman says.

"And we have the government asking people to give more of what they have, dipping into their incomes to support a government that wastes more and more of their money.

"Thank God this time what happened in Vegas didn't stay in Vegas."

* * * *

R. arrives at his office with a lingering hangover from yesterday's hearings and the merriment that went along with watching them.

He opens the shades in hopes that the punishing sunlight will spur him on. To enhance his solar power he decides to make an espresso with his new machine.

There's a knock on the door just as R. hits the 'start' button. He turns around and is pleased to see an attractive woman at the threshold.

"Good afternoon, sir. Are you—"

"Yes, the name on the door is mine," R. says.

"Oh good. I'm Emily from the Ethics Department. I wanted to speak with you about something that came to our attention recently."

"Okay, sure. Have a seat. Would

114

you like an espresso?"

"Oh, thank you. Yes, please."

"So what has 'come to your attention'?"

"It seems you recently purchased an airline ticket."

"Yes," R. says.

"Well, I wanted to speak to you about that purchase," Emily says.

"Okay."

"I understand that you did not purchase them from the GovTravel site. Is that correct?"

R. nods.

"Okay, well, I wanted to verify the source you ultimately used..."

"Expedia."

"...and be sure they are not on our list of illegal sources—"

"I got the ticket on Expedia—"

"It's very important that we maintain our ethical standards—"

"Ethics? I saved over five hundred dollars!" *I can't believe I made her an espresso*, R. thinks.

"Uh, what? You *saved* money? Gosh, they didn't mention that in my report. Oh, this is really serious," Emily says as she writes furiously.

Emily gives R. a stern disappointed school teacher look and

115

says, "Sir, who authorized you to save the government money?"

"It's not the government's money. It's the taxpayers'. Did you miss the hearings?"

"You know, I never thought of it that way." Emily says, chewing on the idea for a moment.

"But sir this will require further investigation," she finally says.

As Emily speaks R. takes a final sip of his espresso then gently puts the cup down. He stands up and removes his suit jacket from the hangar behind the door.

Emily says, "So, I have additional questions to ask you..."

R. quietly picks up his Economist magazine and starts walking towards the door. Emily stands up to follow him into the corridor.

"Sir, there are more questions...where are you going?"

R. keeps walking but looks over his shoulder and says, "I'm going home."

"Just going home?" Emily says.

"Yeah, it's Friday."

50148131R00074

Made in the USA
Columbia, SC
02 February 2019